"...a delight to the eye and the ear."
—*School Library Journal*

DO PENGUINS DREAM?

A book about what we like to think a penguin likes to think about.

—Vivian Walsh & J.otto Seibold, the creators
of the bestselling **OLIVE, THE OTHER REINDEER**

PENGUIN STORY

"they Fly
in the water"

THEADORA WALSH, AGE 3, 1995

PENGUIN DREAMS

dedicated to
all of
THE BABIES.

Penguin Dreams

J. Otto Seibold and V. L. Walsh

chronicle books · san francisco

Shhhhhh...

Chongo Chingi is

SLEEPING

But even when sleeping,
sleeping,
a penguin keeps
thinking.

Chongo Chingi is

DREAMING

Thoughts are flying
round and round,
thoughts of flying
off the ground.

"Icicle-barnicle,
what shall we do?"

"We'll meet in the water!"
and off they flew.

One to the water,
one to the air...

Chongo didn't know he could go up there.

honk-honk

BEEP-BEEP

FLUTTER

EEEP!

FLUTTER

You can't count on a bat
to stay just that.

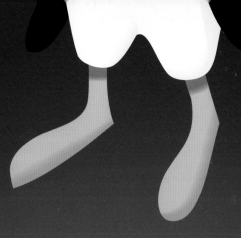

Space is no trouble...

CHONGO
CHONGO
CHONGO

oook-ook

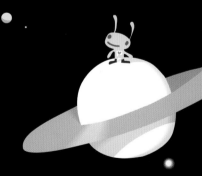

...if you float like a bubble.

**Ring-aling-ling...
Ding-dong-dingi...
Time to wake-up
Chongo Chingi!**

First paperback edition published in 2005 by Chronicle Books LLC.

Book design by J.otto Seibold.
Typeset in Honky and Rosewood.
The illustrations in this book were rendered on an
Apple computer Power Macintosh 8500/120. Using Adobe
Illustrator v6.0 software.
Manufactured in China.
ISBN 0-8118-5100-1

The Library of Congress has catalogued the previous edition
as follows:
Seibold, J.otto.
Penguin dreams / J.otto Seibold and V.L. Walsh.
p. cm.
Summary: Chongo Chingi the penguin has a dream in which he
experiences the excitement of flying, but then he must wake up.
ISBN 0-8118-2558-2
[1. Penguins —Fiction. 2. Flight —Fiction. 3. Stories in rhyme.]
I. Walsh, Vivian. II. Title.
PZ8.3.S457Pe   1999
[E]—dc21   99-16586
CIP

Distributed in Canada by Raincoast Books
9050 Shaughnessy Street, Vancouver, British Columbia V6P 6E5

10 9 8 7 6 5 4 3 2

Chronicle Books LLC
85 Second Street, San Francisco, California 94105

www.chroniclekids.com

beak

belly

eyes

flippers

boots

orange

white

blue

black

tangerine

J.otto Seibold and V. L. Walsh

POLAR EXPLORERS

are currently holed up in
Ice Base: San Francisco

USA

Praise for

Olive, the Other Reindeer

"...a memorable ride."
—The New York Times

"...very funny." —Booklist

"...this reindeer game exudes
contemporary Christmas spirit."
—★Publishers Weekly, starred review

"...the art sings a song all its own."
—Kirkus Review